THINGS

THINGS

Alfonso R Castelao

Translated by
Kirsty Hooper, Isabel Mancebo Portela, Craig
Patterson and Manuel Puga Moruxa
(of the Oxford Centre for Galician Studies)

PLANET

First published
in Wales in 2001
by Planet

PO Box 44
Aberystwyth
Ceredigion SY23 3ZZ
Cymru/Wales
e-mail: planet.enquiries@planetmagazine.org.uk

Designed by Glyn Rees

Printed by Gwasg Gomer,
Llandysul, Ceredigion

The publishers gratefully acknowledge
the financial support of the
Consellería de Cultura e Comunicación Social
of the Xunta de Galicia

Esta obra foi subvencionada pola Consellería de Cultura e Comunicación Social, Dirección Xeral de Promoción Cultural na convocatoria de subvencións para 1996.

ISBN 0 9505188 8 3

Contents

Introduction

The artist and politician Alfonso Daniel Rodríguez Castelao (1886-1950) was born in the small fishing village of Rianxo on the western coast of Galicia, the rain-washed, windswept corner of Spain.

Forced to emigrate out of hardship like so many other Galicians of the nineteenth and twentieth centuries, at the age of nine the young Castelao left for the Argentinian pampas. Exile — whether economic or political — was an aspect of Castelao's life that was reflected and explored in his art, as was the constant threat of blindness that plagued him and the premature death of his son. Returning to Galicia five years later at the turn of the century, Castelao studied to be a doctor in Santiago de Compostela, later abandoning the medical profession to pursue his artistic vocation, a path that also led to involvement in the political process. As well as an artist, writer, cartoonist, caricaturist, novelist and playwright, Castelao became one of the fathers of modern Galician nationalism, a model politician whose sense of ethics and humanity won him unprecedented respect not only in Galicia, but also in the political and cultural arena of Spain. From 1916, when he joined the burgeoning nationalist movement, his name, indeed his entire artistic output, became indivisible from political commitment. Although he claimed never to have been a professional politician, he recognised the clear political and ideological vocation that the content of his works expressed. Twice a member of the Spanish parliament and leader of the Galician Nationalist Party from 1931 until the outbreak of civil war, Castelao was also a member of Galicia's first major unified intellectual grouping, the Xeración Nós (or the 'We Generation'), which sought to re-assess Galician culture, identity and history after many centuries of decadence.

As only one of two politicians representing purely Galician interests in the parliament in Madrid, Castelao rose to the forefront of the nationalist cause. He campaigned for the official recognition of Galician and bilingual status for Galicia, the improvement of social conditions and, above all, a self-governing Galicia within a federal Iberian Republic. In Galicia, a statute of autonomy was finally approved in 1936 by an overwhelming majority in a universal plebiscite. However, civil war erupted nineteen days later, preventing the statute from being ratified; in Madrid as part of a delegation to oversee the document's endorsement by parliament, Castelao did not fall victim to the immediate repression that ensued in Galicia, where most of his colleagues were summarily executed, imprisoned, persecuted or exiled. Through his artwork and diplomatic travails, Castelao went on to play an enormous role in the defence of democracy in Spain both during and after the Civil War, a task that took him to Cuba, the U.S.A. and the U.S.S.R. Finally settling in Buenos Aires in 1940, Castelao worked tirelessly as the leader of Galicia's exiled community and member of the Republican government-in-exile until his death from lung cancer in 1950. His remains were finally brought back to a recently instituted democratic, bilingual and autonomous Galicia in 1984, and rest today in Santiago de Compostela.

Galicia, on the isolated Atlantic fringe of Spain, claims a contentious Celtic legacy in its strong bagpipe tradition, a love of poetry and music, an affinity with Nature, a bent for melancholy and a preoccupation with mortality. Whilst Celtic credentials are somewhat clouded in the mists of pre-history, what is certain is that frequent famines (like the last great one of 1853-54) and poverty were the reasons why so many Galicians left their homeland, and why many comparisons are drawn today with Celtic regions to the north. Geography also meant that Galicia was one of the kingdoms where the cultural effects of the seven hundred year Moorish presence in Spain were least felt, linguistically or religiously. Nevertheless, a strong indigenous and pantheist creed pervaded Galicia until it was rooted out by the early church in the fifth century, although its echoes were never fully silenced. Galicia is traditionally the heartland of witchcraft and magic in Spain, but officially its identity is Catholic and symbolised by the magnificent cathedral at Santiago de Compostela, built to house the supposed relics of the apostle St. James and one of the foremost sites of pilgrimage in medieval Europe. Galicia's political isolation began in the fifteenth century after outbursts of peasant revolt and a a series of ill-favoured power struggles, continued under the rule of Ferdinand and Isabella, and was sealed with the subsequent construction of a Spanish nation state and a vast overseas empire at whose centre was the dominant kingdom of Castile. The influx of modernity, in the forms of industrialisation and urban-isation, was both late and insubstantial.

Castelao's text does not present a static vision of Galician reality during the early part of this century; instead, it is a testament to a vanishing society and its transition to the modern world. During the first decades of the twentieth century, traditional Galicia was under-going a decisive transformation and period of social change. The squirearchy was slowly becoming a defunct part of Galicia's social and political patterns, its place being taken by the urban bourgeoisie, and modernity's effects on traditional ways of life had never been so apparent. Nevertheless, Galicia was still largely a rural country with poor communications and scarce localised industry, a semi-feudal backwater that had hardly changed in centuries. The comparison with Ireland is an accurate one: the ruling minority consist-ed of largely absentee landlords (the clergy and the petty rural aristocracy) and a small urban bourgeoisie; political hegemony was maintained by petty tyranny and vote rigging by local political bosses. The peas-antry made up the vast majority of the Galician popu-lation, and was gradually attaining ownership of the land whilst struggling for subsistence amidst agrarian backwardness caused by a medieval system of land dis-tribution and management that desperately needed reform. This deprivation is captured in stories about the 'little Duchess', old Fanchuca, and the playlet in two scenes. For countless numbers, emigration was the only alternative to extreme hardship and poverty, and again this social concern is addressed by *Things*, notably through the characters of Bieito, Doña Carmen, Panchito and, perhaps most poignantly, Migueliño's father. Some estimates suggest that one in three Galicians have been forced to emigrate during the past five centuries, and from the beginning of the last century until the 1960's, large waves of Galicians have sought a better life abroad, mostly in Latin America and industrial Europe.

During the 1920's and 1930's, Galician society was increasingly divided along class lines, and polarised into the urban and the rural, the modern and the traditional, the non-Galician and the Galician, the haves and have nots. In *Things*, social division and inequality are reflected in characters from the periphery of society and the human (as well as animal) condition, and the text itself played an enormous part in helping to increase awareness of the need to actively improve Galician society and culture, reflecting Castelao's ethical commitment to Galicia. As a politician, Castelao actively sought to bring Galicia into the modern world without compromising unique aspects of her cultural identity; as a writer, he implicitly encourages the reader to cast a cautionary eye over modernity and its effects on human dignity, community and tradition.

Galicia had its own important literary tradition in the later Middle Ages, when its language was the principal medium of lyrical poetry throughout the Iberian kingdoms, even when written by Castilian court poets. But that tradition had faded by the start of the sixteenth century, and it was only with Romanticism, and its interest in the revaluation of cultural diversity, that interest in Galician cultural and literary traditions developed after several centuries of cultural and political repression. This prompted the Rexurdimento, a literary and cultural revival epitomised from the 1860's to the 1890's by the poets Rosalía de Castro, Eduardo Pondal and Curros Enríquez, and the historian Manuel Murguía. The Xeración Nós (1918-1936) represented the subsequent phase of this rebirth of Galician literary and artistic culture. As a key member of this intellectual group, Castelao played a major role in the creation of a national literature firmly linked to European tradition and the artistic avant-garde, that sought to bypass artistic mediation through Madrid, traditionally the centralist broker of imported culture in Spain.

The short pieces that make up *Things* were published in magazines during the twenties and thirties. The first collection was published in book form in 1926, and the second in 1929, before being gathered into a single volume in 1934. It became Castelao's most popular work, making him the most well known intellectual and artist in Galicia during his lifetime and beyond. There is a lot more to *Things* than meets the eye... At the beginning of what at first may seem to be a hotchpotch of narrative vignettes, Castelao elaborates upon his decision to write as distinct to the exclusive pursuit of the plastic arts: the human eye and the paintbrush are less capable of capturing the reality of that which lies behind the purely visual. This is the great philosophical concern of Castelao and his text, and is expressed in deceptively simple terms. *Things* attests to the need for artistic perception to reach beyond appearance, to the need for all art to evoke more than an image or word, and to convey emotion in every sense that suggests solidarity and the need for national self-esteem: to be committed to something beyond the parameters of art itself. This is ultimately the key to the work's universality, and its ability to work on a number of different levels. It is reinforced by Castelao's characteristic use of sketches: there is a unity of expression between text and image that is essential to Castelao's art and which is exemplified in *Things*. Text elaborates upon the poignant impact of the image, whilst image permits greater economy of expression: more is said by saying less.

More than any of his contemporaries, Castelao's great gift lay in finding the perfect equilibrium between aesthetics and social commitment. Whilst *Things* exemplifies the fecund plasticity of his prose, its beauty, poetic sensibility and infinite suggestiveness, it is not art for art's sake, but part of a political agenda awakened by nationalist cause: committed literature that sought a committed reader. Far from the sentimental and provincial literature of customs and manners through which Galicia had often been contemplated in the past, Castelao's contribution to the modernisation of Galician prose involved an implicit appeal for a reader able to respond to his depiction of national defects as well as virtues, to collective afflictions and hopes. And the tool for this task is humour, or Galician retranca: the deadpan statement of the obvious; the subtle irony of understatement; the dark, corrosive and macabre humour that Castelao wielded so well. This is the humour of those small countries that have lost out in history, of the colonised and the conquered, and Castelao had begun a previous work with the words of Mark Twain: 'Beneath humour there is always great sorrow'. In spite of the simple, improvised appearance of *Things*, Castelao polished his writings repeatedly in order to achieve, largely through humour, the necessary effects of bathos and the absurd, often stepping into the fictional world as narrator to distance the reader from the action: these dual effects of irony and alienation look back to Socrates and anticipate Brecht respectively. They also gave new legitimacy and impulse to the wider perception of Galician as an authentic narrative medium.

Since its decline as a literary language, Galician had been preserved in the speech of the mostly illiterate peasantry and fishing communities. Castilian was the language of social and cultural prestige, of the bourgeoisie and declining squirearchy that slowly abandoned the country for the city during the second half of the nineteenth century. This was perceived as progress, whereas rural Galicia, with her traditional culture and what was seen as a peasant dialect, was increasingly stigmatised for its backwardness. In spite of the literary revival of the later nineteenth century, it was Castelao and his generation that made the first decisive step in ending Galician's subservience to Castilian in all spheres of language use.

Because of his background, Castelao was the only

member of the Xeración Nós that grew up speaking Galician as the everyday language of communication, rather than cultivating it simply on account of later political commitment. His literary language is therefore rooted in the heritage of his childhood, and this is reflected in his approach to presenting a model for standardised Galician, a task in which all Galician writers were involved, but which lacked consolidated and collective scientific rigour to achieve definitive results at the time. As a writer participating in the conscientious differentiation of Galician from Castilian, he did not indulge in linguistic engineering by employing archaisms, erudite words or fashioning neologisms like the majority of his colleagues. Instead, his prose is one of economic agility, purity and precision, intertwining everyday language with highly original poetic expression. Whilst owing a great deal to his medical and artistic eye, the language of *Things* reflects Castelao's debt to the oral preservation of Galician in its attention to the reader and in maintaining a measured narrative pace, in its reproduction of personal and collective anecdotes, its style and patterns of delivery.

Many of the stories told to Castelao as a child by his grandmother became material for the enigmatic and poetic prose we find in this small work; it is both from and for the storytelling tradition, Castelao's contribution to the preservation of a popular art form from which he drew so much. Whilst retaining all of its evocative simplicity and powerful concision, Galician is ennobled in *Things*, invested with power and highly original poetic intensity that is strengthened by a sense of rhythm and deliberate suppression of punctuation that conveys urgency and the importance of what Castelao felt to be the text's reception and message. The language that he inherited from the fishing and farming classes — the repository of popular, traditional Galician culture — and to which he gave artistic impulse as well as accessibility in his writings, was the finest literary model available from the pre-war period that could be drawn upon as a paradigm for the creation of a normative Galician language in the 1980's.

For these reasons, *Things* is a work of true artistic integrity. Castelao's other works are further evidence of his artistic versatility and intellectual concerns. *A Glass Eye: Memoirs of a Skeleton* (*Un ollo de vidro. Memorias dun esquelete*, 1922) is Castelao's first contribution to Galician narrative, a very short novel imbued with Galician humour and a macabre, tragicomic touch that act as a vehicle for social critique. His *Diary* (*Diario*, 1921) and *Stone Crosses of Brittany* (*As Cruces de Pedra na Bretaña*, 1930) are the products of a sabbatical spent in European cities and their museums, and an artistic journey to Brittany respectively; both works reflect the Europeanising vein of Castelao and his generation. Castelao's only novel, *The Same Old Two* (*Os dous de sempre*, 1934), pivots on two conceptions or ways of living life as embodied by two protagonists: to be or not to be. With humorous shades of the picaresque, it remains one of the most popular examples of Galician narrative to date. *Old Men Should Not Fall In Love* (*Os vellos non deben namorarse*, 1941) is his only play, and draws on the early European symbolist drama of Paul Fort's Théatre d'Art and the theatre of Nikita Balief's Moscovite company in its integral use of dance, painting, speech, music and mime. *Always in Galicia* (*Sempre en Galiza*, 1944) is an extended essay, the synthesis of Castelao's vision of Galician nationhood, and is today considered a veritable bible of Galician nationalism.

At the heart of *Things* is the Galician concept of enxebrismo, or the authentic, quintessentially Galician. However, part of the avowed aim of the Xeración Nós was to make of Galicia 'a cell of universality', and it is by intellectualising popular culture that Castelao is able to evoke almost as many themes of a universal nature as there are 'things' to talk about. In fact, most of the big questions are to be found in this text of succinct economical intensity: the relativity of truth and objectivity; life and death; innocence and experience; and, of course, love. A group translation has allowed a notoriously culture-specific work in a minority language to express these themes accurately in English. A combination of perspectives, both Galician and English, has allowed *Things* to retain all of its power of expression on the converging planes of cultural experience that are the local and the universal, and there can be few texts that couple these in so economical a fashion. It is a unique written artefact of a world in transition, an oral tradition and the unenviable task of hauling a culture out of the mire of history's fickleness. *Things* is also a window onto that culture and its role in shaping the Galician reality of today, and it is hoped that this translation contributes in some way to the ongoing exposure of Galicia and her culture as a vibrant, unique voice that merits attention on the wider scale that Castelao hoped for and envisaged.

Craig Patterson

Translators' Acknowledgements

Our thanks go to Editorial Galaxia and to Planet for their help in the preparation of this translation, and most of all to John Rutherford, Director of the Centre for Galician Studies, The Queen's College, Oxford, for his thoughtful suggestions.

CLOSE TO NATURE

This is the moment when the earth, to get to sleep, begins to turn its back on the light, and the smoke from the rooftops, thick and milky, begins to spread out along the bottom of the valley. There is nothing out of this world about painting what the eye, which will be eaten by worms, can see; yet there are more things in the landscape worth our attention, for inside that singing water-mill two lovers are kissing for the first time and inside that pazo by the dead chestnut tree the dogs are howling.

From a churchyard we can see the valley sunk in rain. The water, falling without respite, lays the blue smoke flat against the shining rooftiles of a hut. The lanes are covered in mud and a blanket seller rides past on his beast of burden. Here is a subject for a painter; but there is still more to the landscape, for they are tolling for the dead in the church belfry and the sound is as bitter as if they were striking the bell with the head of the deceased and we cannot tell in which of the village houses there has been a tragedy, because each and every one of them is sad.

A moonlit night. Beside a legendary crossroads the base of a cruceiro is the stone table where they place the dead to say a response for them;

through the pines the peaceful ria appears; the moon hangs from the branch of a pine. The painter has to evoke something more than what he can see, because on the cruceiro's stone table, that same day at dusk, they placed the dead body of a young man back from military service; along that hollow way goes a student priest brooding over the girl with the red headscarf who robbed him of his vocation. And in the distance people are singing an alalá.

S unday at dawn. The faraway woods are tinged with the azures of Patinir; the broom and the gorse add their yellow notes to the divine green symphony of the landscape. There are many more things in the landscape for an artist, because on a branch of that apple tree Guerra Junqueiro's blackbird, still "gleaming and jovial", awaits the village priest to wish him good morning; it rained yesterday; the church bells ring out a muiñeira and along the river-meadow paths down there the little black and red ants are coming to mass.

T ime has adorned the old feudal castle with a layer of gold and silver; the slaves of the taxman are hoeing their plots of maize; through the shadowy willows at the bottom of the valley the sickle of the river can be glimpsed. The sun beats the back of the earth. It is all waiting to be painted, for it all delights the eye; yet in this landscape there is still more. Today is St John's Eve, there is the scent of a mother's lap in the air, the crickets are singing and the warm wind brings us the sound of a tuba from afar. Tomorrow we shall wash with scented herbs.

N ight was falling. The black silhouette of a pine tree was sketched out against the dark blue of the sky. You all know that in spring pine trees sprout thousands of candles, taking on the appearance of giant candelabra. How often have we felt the urge to light the candles on the pine trees! Well then, the village viaticum (the priest, two boys, four women praying) happened to pass close to my pine tree; and then came the miracle! Brother pine, sensing the holiness of the moment and in homage to the Sacred Host, lit his candles, which remained alight until the viaticum was lost past the bend in the lane.

O ne Christmas Day, while contemplating a landscape that resembled a Nativity, I realised that there is more beauty in the little flowers of the fields than in garden flowers. The daring little flowers that spring up in the fields look as if they might have been created by Bosch or by Breughel the Elder, whereas the dusty garden flowers look like Rubens' blubbery nudes. Ever since then I have wanted to be an adventurer of letters.

T hey call her the *Little Duchess* and her tiny feet have always been bare.

She goes for water, she peels potatoes, and they call her the *Little Duchess*.

She has never been to school for want of a blouse to put on, and they call her the *Little Duchess*.

She has never tasted any sweets save for a sugar cube, and they call her the *Little Duchess*.

Her mother is so poor that she works as a daily menial in the Duke's house.

And they call her the *Little Duchess*!

A forgotten lane that no longer leads anywhere. A lane paved with stone, infested with tangled brambles and stinging nettles, which disappears into the dark mouth of a hollow way.

I always used to be asking my grandmother: "Where does the Old Track go?"

And my grandmother would answer mysteriously: "It doesn't go anywhere, little one."

That Old Track kept beckoning to me, and once I was grown up I ventured down it. And beyond the fearful hollow way I came across a deserted village.

Farmhouses of fine stone, wine presses evoking

abundance, rotten beams, heaps of rooftiles; everything shrouded in ivy, brambles and laurel, and above that lush vegetation the red and yellow leaves of a vine with no fruit.

I sat down beneath a dead walnut tree to pick over feelings that are there even today, waiting...

When I returned home I heard the story of the forgotten village from my grandmother.

"What happened was that the locals, taken to thieving, burgled the monastery of Armenteira."

Waiting for the right moment to share out the wealth their leader buried it in a secret place; but the next day the leader was found dead in his bed and nothing more was ever known of that treasure.

Afterwards all was misfortune. The pairs of oxen died, the crops failed, the children died of rickets, the springs dried up. To drive away the evil spell they erected cruceiros everywhere.

It was to no avail. In the end all was known, and even today the village is cut off from honest people.

W herever there is a cruceiro there has been a sin, and each cruceiro is a prayer in stone that has brought a pardon down from Heaven, because of the repentance of whoever paid for it and the deep feeling of whoever made it.

Have you ever stopped to look at our village cruceiros? Well you should, you know.

The Virgin of Sorrows, carved deep into the back of many stone crosses, is not the Pietà of sculptors; it is the Piedade created by the stonemasons.

Our stonemasons, letting themselves be guided by feeling, could not imagine a man on his mother's lap.

For the stonemason artists, Jesus Christ is always tiny, always the Child, because he is the Son, and we sons are always tiny on our mothers' laps.

Look at the cruceiros and you will discover many treasures.

S crapper was a fisherman who earned masses of
money that stayed in his pocket just like water in
a sieve. On land *Scrapper* had no brains at all; as
soon as he set foot in his boat he became a sage. He
had many children and many grandchildren and all
of them spent and spent because the sea provided for
everything.

Nobody denied him the reputation he enjoyed as a
good skipper and a good Christian; but at times he did
seem to have dealings with the devil. Other fishermen
would cast out their tackle and not catch a thing;
along would come *Scrapper* and catch fish galore.

Scrapper was generous by nature. Once on the verge of drowning he offered himself to Our Lady and gave her a cloak worth six thousand reás, as well as a sung mass, music, fireworks, new clothes and food aplenty.

Scrapper had faith in his good fairy. Once he fell ill and his eldest son acted as skipper. The moment the son came back from sea he went to his father's bedside and stuttering with fear told him that the tackle was all lost, caught on some rocks. *Scrapper* simply said: "Don't worry, Ramón; the sea took it away, the sea will provide for some more." And then he fell silent and turned towards the wall.

Scrapper had such trust in the sea!

But all this abundance suddenly came to an end and hunger entered every home. That happened when the dragnets killed off the old ways of fishing.

Scrapper appeared one day before my father, a friend of his since childhood, and an advisor too.

"You know something?" he said. "There's hunger — hunger! — in *Scrapper's* house. You know very well that I've never asked anybody for anything; but now I've come knocking at your door to borrow a thousand reás. I want to put a new balcony on my house, see, and that way the people who notice that

I'm doing some building work won't think that my lot have nothing to put in their mouths."

My father, who has seen the world, assured him that hunger is cured with bread; but *Scrapper* stood firm and spoke again:

"Shame is worse than hunger."

And my father, knowing that he could not convince on land a man who is intelligent only at sea, opened the drawer and took out a thousand reás; but *Scrapper* stopped him:

"No, don't give them to me now; I'll come for them later."

That evening you should have heard the crowd of people that came to our house. It was *Scrapper* coming with his wife, his children, his sons-in-law, his daughters-in-law and all of his grandchildren to collect the thousand reás.

Scrapper's mob filled the house and it was frightening to imagine them surrounding their patriarch and demanding bread.

Scrapper, with his cap pulled down over his ears, asked my father for the money, and on receiving it from his hands took his cap off religiously and showing the money to everybody said in a solemn voice:

"My dear wife and children: if I die you know that fifty pesos are owed to this man."

And without another word he donned his cap and went off ahead of everyone, down the stairs.

O n the night of the last novena of All Souls the church was infested with fears.

A soul shone in each candle and the souls that could not find any room in the lighted candles huddled away in the shadowy corners and from there they stared at the children and made faces at them.

Each flame that the sacristan snuffed out was a lighted soul that vanished in strands of smoke and all of us could hear the breathing of the souls in each candle that died.

Ever since then the smell of wax has brought back the memory of the fears of that night.

The priest was singing the response before a coffin full of bones and the moment the paternoster died away the keening started.

Four men came forward pushing aside women crazy with grief and with one hand they raised the coffin and with the other they clutched torches.

The procession came to an end at the ossuary in the churchyard. The four men were carrying the coffin suspended just off the ground and the torches tilted dripping wax over the bones. Behind followed the swarm of women letting out deafening wails, more chilling still than those of the keening at a funeral for the drowned. And if the women were bawling the men were shedding silent tears.

In that procession everybody had someone to cry for and everybody was crying.

And even Baltasara was crying, a girl raised on everyone's charity who had been found in a basket, next to a cruceiro, and who had no father or mother, nor anyone to cry for; but she caught the wailing bug and she too bawled and bawled with all her might.

On the way back to the village, a neighbour asked the girl:

"Who were you crying for, Baltasara?"

And she sobbed:

"Do you think that having nobody to cry for is such a small misfortune, señora?"

T he old bridge can no longer bear the loves and
the tragedies it carries on its back and soon it
will collapse overnight.

If the old bridge were to speak it could bear
witness to what I am about to tell you.

There was a girl, fair-skinned and beautiful as the
daughter of a king. Because of her frailty and her
noble bearing they made her a seamstress and every
night at dusk she would walk over the old bridge and
cross paths with the lad who was studying to be a
priest.

"Good evening, Rosa."

"Good evening, Pedro."

She would be coming from her sewing; he would

be returning from his Latin. And they looked at each other so often as they passed on the old bridge that by the time Pedro entered the Seminary he was carrying a love in his heart.

Winter passed and Pedro came back from his studies and he was burning to see Rosa. The young lover would sit on the old bridge every night at dusk, waiting...

The fair-skinned and beautiful seamstress no longer did any sewing and whenever they met by chance on some road she hid her face in her headscarf and he felt like dying.

One day, with his heart in turmoil, Pedro overheard a conversation on the bridge.

"That pretty little face of hers has turned into a hideous mask. Her father came from folk marked with a cross in the parish book, you know, so there's no hope of a cure... What poor little Rosa's got, see, is leprosy..."

That day, night closed in for Pedro as if all the doors in the world were closing.

Now he is an old and saintly priest who often sits on the old bridge at dusk to share out the gift of his saintliness among all who pass by.

I n Martiño's dark mind a firefly always flickered. Martiño longed to be the master of the church belfry.

He grew up hanging on the sacristan's coat-tails to win him over and, moving up in life, he was made bellringer, for Martiño was a halfwit and obsessed with ringing bells.

At first, Martiño used to scare children away. Then the belfry door, normally open, acquired a latch. Shortly after that, Martiño put a lock on it and shut himself in.

This was how Martiño entered surreptitiously into possession of the church belfry and made it his home and the bells the tools with which he worked for his own ends.

We boys never recognised his right to rule in the belfry and we challenged him for it with loathing and with fear, since all those who played a prank on him paid double when they went into the church, which was the mousetrap in which Martiño caught boys.

We were so desperate to climb up to the belfry that our imaginations never stopped plotting. One day we hatched such a good scheme that we managed to get in. Needless to say, in poor Martiño's *House* we did not leave a thing whole or unharmed. And it was then that Martiño began to lure us to him in order to take his revenge.

As we sat all agog in the churchyard, Martiño would tell us, in a fearsome voice, of the things that had happened in the belfry, when the souls of the Santa Compaña walked over his chest, when one night the bells were pealed and he went to see who was ringing them and was slapped on the face... We never stirred as we listened dumbstruck to Martiño's tales, and as night fell we would be dying of fright.

Martiño's revenge was such that I still suffer from it today in these terrors that assail me.

I had not yet been born and my mother was a girl. At nightfall on a mild April day the people of my town saw a ray of light coming in from the sea, striking the church belfry like a ray of sun that had stolen its way through a breach in the clouds; yet it was not of sun nor of moon nor of anything of the kind. It was a light of lightning-bolts, cast down by a watchful eye, searching for something, pausing every so often on the church belfry to find out the time and then resume its work.

People were flocking in from all corners of the town and they took over the square, as quiet as mice. With their feet planted on the ground they followed the movement of the light with their eyes; they were breathing slowly and their hearts were beating hard.

Well into the night the doctor, a man of great

scientific repute, arrived and everybody went over to him expecting the truth to issue from his mouth. The doctor looked at the light, wrinkled his nose, shrugged his shoulders and said with a frosty expression on his face:

"I am not familiar with this phenomenon."

Never had he said such a thing before. One woman expressed everybody's fear in an anguished shriek. And the crazed people scattered through the streets shouting: *It's the end of the world! It's the end of the world!*

Some ran with sacks of grain on their backs towards the woods, others kneeled at the cruceiros and prayed. Little children carried by their mothers cried with all their might; the elderly begged for confession.

Thieves returned their plunder or admitted to their plundering; slanderers tugged at their victims' clothes imploring forgiveness. In the face of death all were bewailing their sins.

And the terrifying cries echoed on into the night, like cock-crows: *It's the end of the world! It's the end of the world!*

The old priest could not confess sinners fast enough and, by now exhausted, he decided to bless and absolve them all at once, for death was close and there was no time to lose.

And now Ramón, the strongest lad in town, arrived leading his beloved by the hand. The pair of lovers drove their way through the crowd like an iron nail and presented themselves before the priest and fell at his feet.

"Marry us, sir, marry us, we're living in mortal sin."

And before the priest had finished blessing them a voice was heard saying:

"There's no need to be afraid, it's only electric light from the English fleet! Don't be afraid, it's only electric light!"

It was the owner of the fish-salting factory, come running with a lantern in his hand.

Ramón and Micaela were no longer living in sin and felt ashamed before all the people.

I n Tub Cove there lives — so the story goes — an enchanted lady who comes in the early morning to comb her hair on the rocks of the shore, and I liked to go and kill time in that fearful solitude, hoping that the beauty that so many sailors had seen would appear before my eyes. And I spent days and days sitting on top of the same rock, on the lookout for the enchanted lady.

I began to forget about the enchantment and got used to the frightening solitude and the roar of the waves of the sea. I still carry in my ears the sound of the waves breaking against the rocks and the reply that the rocks made at the bottom of Tub Cove.

My eyes seldom scanned the horizon: rather they lingered over the depths of the water, where I could glimpse the world that has created myths in the popular imagination.

I don't know why, but my gaze always came to rest on a stone that was round like a skull, covered all over in green seaweed. And soon my visits had no purpose other than to gaze at the round stone.

One spring-tide day the sea ebbed so far that the stone stuck its crown out of the water and it had never looked so much like a skull covered in green hair. Each time a wave lapped over the stone the hair frayed out in the sea, floating like the locks of a drowned woman. Whenever the wave receded the stone emerged from the water and the hair settled and then it seemed as if it had been combed with a centre parting, exactly like a woman's head.

I often watched how the waves of the sea played with the green locks and my enchanted eyes never grew tired of the sight.

One misty evening I was tempted to pick the stone up and ruffle its locks, just to put my mind at ease.

Risking my neck I managed to come close to the round stone and stretching out my arm I grabbed the locks and pulled.

The stone was light and I raised it in the air like an executioner displaying a severed head.

Whenever I remember I still feel a chill in my spine. What I had hanging by its locks was not a stone, no: it was... a human skull!

Perhaps the skull of the enchanted lady, who must have died, for it has been a long time now since she has come in the early morning to comb her hair on the rocks of the shore.

RAMÓN CARBALLO

I

When I was a boy Ramón Carballo turned up; he was wearing a hemp jacket lined with red felt and a cap with a tortoiseshell peak, like someone going to sea. And his chest was tattooed, for I clearly saw a bird with a letter in its beak and his name underneath.

I remember that Ramón Carballo went to Buenos Aires and came back penniless. Next he went to Havana and didn't bring back any money. Later he went to New York and came back just as poor as when he'd left. And then Ramón Carballo went who knows where and never came back at all.

II

Here one should really write a novel, but I am a man of honour and I must not tell what I do not know. But a novel there is in all of this.

III

M. Lavalet earns his crust selling human remains. M. Lavalet is a fearsome man: glassy bloodshot eyes, dead hairs like those of an old wig, dried-up streams of filthy sweat on his forehead, the chill of having the substance of many poisons on his hands and on his lips.

This man lives on the third floor in a narrow street in Paris.

One day I knocked at his door and went in... A room full of human bones, some still fresh, comprised the *emporium* for doctors. In the *curiosités* room, for cosmopolitan sorts, there were many things: a mummified foetus staring at its belly button, a gorilla's skull with its warrior-helmet crest, a Chinaman's scalp ready to be placed on a plaster bust.

When M. Lavalet found out that I was an artist he showed me a large collection of tattooed human skins, tanned to make pouches, wallets...

One of the skins was from a man's chest, depicting a bird with a letter in its beak, and below the drawing was emblazoned this name: Ramón Carballo.

T he carrier's only possessions are a nag, a pack-saddle and a stall, and no one can work out how he manages to keep the nag alive. When I think about the carrier's nag, everybody's poor nag, I am reminded of a featherless seagull. That wretched animal, on the verge of degenerating into a donkey, stumbles along at the roadside, close against the brambles, and anyone who makes a journey on this beast of burden will spend the rest of his life on foot.

The wind whistles through the carrier's poor nag.

When some traveller's horse has to spend the night in the carrier's stall, he who can give nothing because he owns nothing enquires with all the airs of the landlord of a well-stocked inn:

"What would you like me to give you, horse? Shall I give you clover, green barley, vetch... or what?"

The carrier isn't exactly a thief, but he's not averse to a little petty pilfering.

One moonlit night off went the carrier towards the cemetery armed with a sickle and a basket. And on arriving at the cemetery wall he threw the basket inside and started to scramble up. As he did so he heard the basket fall back on to the road... The carrier had a mind to run away; but he restrained himself for love of the nag waiting in the stall. He plucked up his courage and grabbing the basket threw it back into the cemetery... Before very long he saw the basket coming back through the air and falling on to the road once more.

Basket in and basket out, while the moon travelled two armspans across the sky.

In a moment of daring the carrier gripped his sickle between his teeth and scrambled up the stones ready to square up to the dead man who kept throwing his basket back. Once he had mounted the wall what met his gaze was the smiling face of his mate *Yellowbelly,* who also used to go to gather grass in the cemetery because he was also a carrier.

And the two friends roared with laughter.

T wo old people who had been young once, too, who had met at a dance, had soon married for love and had lived loving each other totally. Two old people, always together and always silent, who spend their days listening to the chirping of a goldfinch in a cage. Childless and friendless. Alone.

The day before yesterday they took the viaticum to the old man and yesterday he died. His lifelong companion dressed him, shaved him and crossed his hands on his chest.

Today four men came and removed the long coffin with the dead man inside it. The old woman went to the front door and in the loving voice of their days of youth bid farewell to her companion:

"See you soon, Eleuterio!"

And the neighbours who had come to watch the show covered their mouths and laughed from their bellies. The old woman's farewell went the rounds and reached the Gentlemen's Club and *See you soon Eleuterio* became the joke of the moment.

Absolutely everybody laughed and not one of them suspects how sorrowfully the old lover will long for death this winter night.

All those who knew anything of the history of
the town where I was born now rest beneath
the clods. Granny Sinforosa was a little old lady who
went over the ria every day, because she was an
errand-runner by trade, as her mother had been, and
her grandmother, and perhaps all of her foremothers,
ever since those on this side started trading with
those on the other side. She was honest, or seemed
so, for she lived off her reputation as a woman of
honour. Charming and talkative with everyone, she
always had words like carnations in her shrivelled
mouth for the gentlefolk. Granny Sinforosa knew
about all the tragedies in that part of the ria.

On foul-weather days, when the wind hums through the ropes and the spray sweeps the deck of the boat, Granny Sinforosa would withdraw into herself and pray for her soul.

On calm days Granny Sinforosa would pray for the drowned. The boat would be heading for the other side and the errand-runner would be praying and praying.

"Just one Our Father for Xan de Codeso, who drowned one Candlemas Day."

"One Salve Regina for Doña Rosa Faxardo, who threw herself off Falcoeira Point and drowned."

"Just one Our Father, one Salve and one Ave Maria for Belurico's four daughters, who died on the way back from market."

"One Salve for Ramón Collazo, who was carried off by a conger eel and never seen again."

And so she would go on praying, always praying, for all those who have died on that crossing. The old errand-runner stored in her memory the names of the drowned and the dates of the tragedies.

One day I noticed that Granny Sinforosa was praying for *a little boy that died in Tronco*, and I asked her:

"Who was the little boy that died in Tronco, Granny Sinforosa?"

And she replied:

"I don't know, my little darling; that drowning

didn't happen in my time, because my late grandmother, may she rest in Heaven, used to pray for him before me."

Now Granny Sinforosa has died, and nothing is left of all those tragedies except three or four wooden crosses planted among the rocks of the shore. The old errand-runner has carried to the Hereafter the stories of all the drownings of the town where I was born.

Once as I crossed the ria I felt in my breast the emptiness of so much forgetting and in the name of all the drowned I prayed:
Just one Our Father for Granny Sinforosa.

T here was once a Saturday barber who loved
 books that he did not understand and enjoyed
reading them from cover to cover.

Once I found him with his forehead resting on his
hands, in the manner of a thinker, and he said:

"I'm deepening."

And ever since then, for me, there have been men
who deepen.

This Saturday barber went through life with his
senses turned in on his own ignorance, working
alongside a colleague whose senses were open to the
world.

He would often withdraw into himself in order to
deepen into the mysteries of the next life, and would
always end up complaining:

"I can't deepen any more because I don't know Latin."

One day he rested his gaze on the sea — he never took any notice of little things — and after having deepened for a good while he whispered these words into his colleague's ear:

"The sea, you know? The sea... it's a phenomenon!"

The poor Saturday barber astonished everyone with his wisdom... Once he went serious, like one of those toy friars made of wood, and assured his colleague:

"I must die and I must be judged, in spite of I like it or not, don't you know?"

And he spoke with heavy insistence on each syllable of *in spite of I like it or not.*

The Saturday barber would almost always be left with doubts after deepening on things of the next world.

The poor Saturday barber died and they put him in a pine coffin and his colleague went to see him and he shed a tear.

And a woman, one of the keeners, said:

"Now you're not deepening! Now you're not deepening, because now you know everything!"

I was still a country doctor and I was riding up a
lane in the hills. The farmhouses were far away,
the woods too, and there was nothing all around but
gorse and rocks.

At the top of the hill I spotted the figure of a
woman beckoning to me, and the old patriarch
walking alongside my horse told me:

"Poor thing! They call her the *madwoman of the
hills*. She used to be a sensible young girl and as
pretty as a peach and they say it was a witch who put
a spell on her and after losing her mind she had a
baby and they say it was the devil's..."

A crow was circling above the madwoman of the
hills.

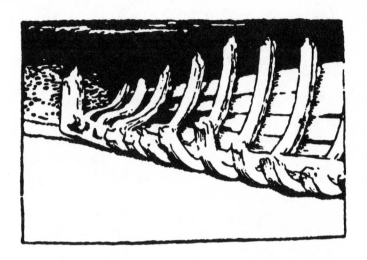

It's still lying there on the beach, the skeleton of that boat, like the backbone of a gigantic fish spat out by the sea.

In the days before all this progress children would play with little boats made of bark, getting used to being sailors, and when they became old men they would play with a real boat, so as not to notice how useless they had become.

The twelve oldest old men in town always had a boat and tackle to play with. They were nicknamed *apostles* because at the Easter Services the priest washed their feet.

On warm sunny days they would cast their tackle out. I am not saying that they caught sufficient fish to sell; but sometimes they did get enough for a stew and then they would swell with pride.

People would venture to forecast good weather with this saying: *tomorrow the apostles' tackle can go to sea*. And nothing wounded the old mens' hearts more.

It was lovely to see them walking in a line carrying their tackle on their backs.

When some gift came their way to remind them of their indigence, they would acknowledge it with dignity: "May people be as good to you when you grow old as you are to us."

We all hesitated to place a crust of maize bread in their hands as one does with landlubbers who beg at doors. Alms are fine for those who are used to receiving them; but a sailor who grows poor because he has grown old would die of shame as he felt the weight of the alms-bag on his back.

Progress has brought wealth and it has brought hunger. The *apostles* have died out and the old people of today go begging at the doors of the rich who own boats and do not go to sea.

W hen Bieito was orphaned a relative arrived from the Americas and took him away.

On the day before the journey he walked up the hill road and there, at the very top, he left a ha'penny well hidden. It was the sentimental idea of a twelve-year-old.

Then, in the pampas of Argentina, it was as if a pack of hounds had been set on him, when he still couldn't look after himself in the solitude of those roadless fields. And he suffered great anguish as he learnt to face up to men, biting back the urge to cry.

In exchange for pieces of his spirit Bieito acquired a new outlook and by working without respite he earned ample riches. He married, had children and took root in foreign soil.

The drudgery of his life did not give him leisure for sentimental recollections and it was only after thirty years of struggle that Bieito took a deep breath and managed to turn back towards the past. And now morriña found its way into his ribcage.

Combing the corners of his memory for the forgotten scraps of his happy life as a child, Bieito always ended up thinking about the ha'penny he had left hidden at the top of the hill. And unable to live any longer without visiting his native fields he boarded a boat and arrived in the Homeland.

The forgotten words of our tongue, the moss, the navelworts, the ferns and all the things he came across on his way filled his heart with joy. When he reached the top of the hill his eyes were overflowing with happiness. In the same place where he had left it he found the ha'penny, and there are no words in the world that could give you an idea of Bieito's emotion at that moment. Then he went away to be with his children.

Now Bieito has a ha'penny hanging from his gold watch chain and he has a wound inside his rib box.

I don't pity the boy who watches with the docile gaze of an ox as motor cars pass by his door. I don't feel sorry for the boy who doesn't run after motor cars. However much the boy starves, he will always be happy.

I do pity the boy who gets itchy feet when motor cars pass by his door. I do feel sorry for the boy who does run after motor cars. Restless boys who test their strength on every machine they see will not satisfy their craving for happiness.

The boys of my land always run after motor cars.

I f I were an author I would write a play in two scenes. The playlet would only last ten minutes.

SCENE ONE

The curtain rises to reveal a village cowshed. On the bracken-covered floor there is a dead cow. Standing around the cow are a little old lady, a prematurely aged woman, a handsome young woman, two pretty little girls, an old patriarch and three blond boys. All are crying buckets and wiping their eyes with their hands. All are wailing and saying sad things that make you laugh, the oafish sayings of peasant folk, wretched and covetous, who think that the death of a cow is a major tragedy. The wailing must be funny in a vulgar way, so that the people in the stalls burst with laughter.

And when the toffs are tired of laughing the curtain will fall.

SCENE TWO

The curtain rises to reveal an elegant living-room, decorated in a grand style. On top of a table with bronze feet there is a silver tray, on top of the tray there is a damask cushion, on top of the cushion there is a dead lap-dog. The dead lap-dog will look like a snowflake. Around her a fine fidalga and two fine little fidalgas are crying. All of them are wailing and wiping their tears with lace handkerchiefs. They are all saying, one after the other, the same foolish things that the peasants said around the dead cow, sad sayings that make you laugh, because the death of a lap-dog isn't such a terrible event.

And when the people in the gods are tired of laughing their heads off, the curtain will fall very slowly.

T hat window is not an eye of the house, as windows normally are, since it is only used for a blind man to bask in the sun, the blind man who became rich singing merry ballads alongside tasty-smelling empanadas in the market.

The pustules that nibbled away at the blind man's eyes were a gift from Our Lord. He was not the sort of blind man who goes begging from door to door; nor a city blind man, who weeps on his violin, dragging a finger withered with hunger slowly along the strings. He was just a country-fair blind man, a rascal, a rogue.

Whenever he wants to recall something from his long life he begins by showing that laughing canine tooth planted in his red gums like a solitary gatepost, then he lets out a triumphant guffaw.

"It was around Martinmas."

The blind man who basks in the sun, like a cat, at the window, has savoured with closed eyes every delight that the world has to offer. By the time I saw him he was very, very old and was giving Christian advice to the young. He lived in the bosom of a farmer's family, with a good bed and good bowls of broth.

They say that the blind man called for a simple woman and showed her many gold sovereigns that gleamed in the sun, and wheedled:

"If you took me to die in your house, my treasures would be yours."

And the woman took him in like someone taking in a saint.

The blind man died and now they say that the clipped sovereigns he kept so close about his person were bits of gold-coloured metal...

It was the blind man's last trick.

I t was to follow the dictates of a true love that she left her land and her mother: a land green and plentiful, a mother old and blind.

In the early days Doña Carmen lived happy in the expectation of returning; later the certainty of dying in exile overwhelmed her. Ever since then the poor lady has lived far from the present, drowning in nostalgia, sweet sadness in her smile; in her eyes the restlessness of the deaf and in her delicate hands the uncertainty of the blind. The good lady took root in foreign soil and will die from the sigh that this left in her.

In the early days, when this faithful lover wept and hoped, a letter came bearing bad news and her husband ripped it up. Then lying letters came, sent from time to time by a cousin at the request of Doña Carmen's husband.

"Isn't it good what cousin Roque says about your mother?"

"Yes, yes, it seems like a miracle."

And Roque kept saying that the old lady was alive, and the old lady reached eighty, ninety, a hundred years old... The old people from days gone by last for so long!... But one day cousin Roque died of old age and then no more letters came.

Doña Carmen wept as in the early days and her husband lavished all his love on her and, no longer able to keep up such an enormous lie, he said one night, putting deep feeling into his words:

"I'm sorry, Carmela. Weep as much as you like, dear: your mother has died; she died thirty five years ago today."

A rich man came back from the Americas and brought a little black Cuban boy with him, like someone bringing a monkey, a parrot, a phonograph...

The little black boy grew up in the village, where he learned to speak real Galician, to dance intricate muiñeiras, to let out deafening aturuxos.

One day the rich man died and Panchito changed masters to earn his bread. In time he became a fine young man, with no other blemish than his colour... Although he was as black as the ace of spades, he had enough charm to make himself loved by everyone. In his Sunday best, with a carnation behind his ear and a sprig of mallow in his lapel, he looked just like any young reveller.

One starry night the idea of going out into the world in search of riches sprang up in his mind. Panchito, like all the young men in the village, felt the urge to emigrate. And one morning of great sadness he crawled up the steps of an ocean liner.

Panchito was on his way to Havana and his wet and shining eyes scrutinised the sea for the lands left astern.

In a street in Havana black Panchito bumped into a man from his village and confessed, sobbing:

"Oh, I can't get used to this land of endless sun; I can't get used to these people. It's killing me!"

Panchito returned to the village. He arrived poor and feeble, but he brought back great riches in his heart. He also brought back a straw hat and a white suit...

There was a drowned man in the sea and the seafaring town had sunk into silence and sadness.

The wind had died down, the sea had become still,

the sun had triumphed in the heavens. And the town was not waking up or warming up, as if it were still night, as if the seafaring people were rejecting God's gifts. Daylight obscured by the anguish of tragedy.

On the calm sea boats were coming and going in search of Ramón's body. In the church a woman and a little boy were weeping before the miracle-working Christ.

A week went by in silence and in sadness.

And one morning the boat carrying Ramón's body moored at the quay.

The town wept dreadful tears, and with deep grief they buried the drowned man's body in the churchyard.

And once Ramón had been left in the company of all the parish dead, the town took a deep breath, it revived in hope, and the people started singing again as they went about their daily work.

The earth does not want to lose the body it lends us and fishermen too obey its laws, because they too are of the earth. If it were not so, what better bed for a seafarer than the bottom of the sea!

The old woman never stops celebrating her happiness.

"This girl came down from Heaven to gladden my old age. An angel sent to me by Our Lord. A beautiful little flower born of my body of clay. Oh, what would become of me, alone in the world, with nobody to love me!"

The old woman continues savouring her celebration.

"This daughter of mine is a saint, because her miraculous little hands can ward off sickness and cure wounds. She has filled my night with light and warmed my old age. What would become of me, all on my lonesome, lying down to die in some lane!"

The old woman continues her litany of celebration.

"My body has lost its oars, but here are my girl's oars, sturdy and strong. Now that my arms have grown tired, her arms have taken on the work. Now that the glass in my windows has frosted over, I can still see the way through my daughter's clear eyes. Oh, what would become of me!"

From the old woman's withered lips come words lit up with contentment.

"She used to be my daughter and now she is my mother. What would become of me without this little mother who cares for me! Oh, and when I die I shall have someone to pray to Heaven for me!"

The old woman goes on and on celebrating her happiness.

One day I asked the old woman:
"Who was the father of your daughter?"
And the old woman replied:
"I don't know what he was called, but... blessed be his name!"

R aising an animal to eat it is not right, even if we turn its flesh into our flesh; but lovingly raising an animal only to take it to market seems to me an example of human depravity.

Market day! Money, false oaths and promises, passing donkeys off as horses, peppered-up meals, stale bread, bad wine, crowded bars... The merry hustle and bustle of markets is as deceptive as carnival masks, for beneath the merriment there is sadness in those who sell and fear in those who buy. On market day everyone acts like a fox and no one has his heart in the right place, because everyone believes that honest folk lose money in market deals.

The bleating of the kid goats, who wail like the sickly children of fidalgos, can wound a weak man's heart; the repulsive squealing of the pigs, who screech at the slightest thing, deafens our ears and dissipates all our compassion. Along the street, at the close of the market, flow the streams of animal suffering; but there is still more to markets.

Men go about their business and take no notice of the other suffering, the human suffering of God's animals. The poor desperate cows who call for their young, the poor calves who go to the slaughterhouse calling for their mothers...

I want everybody to hear this story:
Once upon a time there were two oxen who had grown very old and who had worked together all their lives. Their master sold them for slaughter and they had to part for ever... And it is said that at the moment of parting one said to the other:
"Goodbye, my friend, until we meet at Soutomaor."
(At Soutomaor there was a leather market.)

M any years have passed and even today I feel remorse.

Antroido never went by without two masked men coming to my house. Always the same two muck-rakers, with the same masks, the same outfits, the same sayings. They knew a romantic secret from my youth and every year they would come by to blurt it out to my face with the same words, the same oafish guffaws.

The two masked men banged my door-knocker every Antroido Sunday. Every single year on the same day and at the same time. I was dying to find them out; but never could I discover the smallest clue. They would knock, come in, roar out my secret, laugh their heads off and then run away leaving me seething with anger.

One year I offered them some augardente... and I put before them a carafe full of Leroy laxative (a medicine that isn't much used any more). The masked men sniffed the augardente, tried it suspiciously, babbled a few jokes at my expense, cleared their throats and little by little swallowed the entire carafe. Each one took fifteen purges at the very least. They were well served, the poor wretches!

My fun did not last long. Soon after they left, remorse began to gnaw at my conscience. I was a criminal and the cold sweat of repentance was running down my body. I left the house in search of the masked men. I combed bars and private dances and there was no sign of them; I asked many people and no one could give me any information. Dawn on Monday found me still in the street, exhausted, searching for those masked men...

Never again did I set eyes on them. Never! And I was left with tremendous remorse, because... could they have died?

A street in a distant northern port. The bars are
packed with sailors and blast the hot breath of
drunkards out through their doors. People from all
the races in the world, bellowed songs, music from
gruff pianolas, the stench of greasy bodies...

A sailor who speaks French bumps into a sailor
who speaks English. They exchange promises of
eternal friendship, each in his own tongue. And
neither understanding the other they walk along arm
in arm, holding each other up.

The sailor who speaks French and the sailor who speaks English go into a bar run by a fat man. They want to drink themselves senseless together, to become better friends. Perhaps when they're really drunk they'll be able to understand each other!

And when the sailor who speaks English is no longer in control of his body he begins to sing:

> *Lanchiña que vas en vela;*
> *levas panos e refaixos*
> *para a miña Manoela.*

The sailor who speaks French gawps, hugs his friend, and joins in:

> *Lanchiña que vas en vela;*
> *levas panos e refaixos*
> *para a miña Manoela.*

Ayoohoohoo! Both sailors were Galician.

The barman, fat as any true-bred Fleming, watched the two sailors leaving the bar and tears slid down his ruddy cheeks. And then he moaned nostalgically under his breath:

> *¡Lanchiña que vas en vela!*

The barman was Galician too.

O ld *Hedgemustard* spent his life searching for treasure. With the patience of a lottery player old *Hedgemustard* would comb the market ground after the market, and the festa ground after the festa. How many stone walls he scrutinised in search of the pot full of sovereigns! Alas, poor *Hedgemustard* died without finding the coveted treasure, and in the last days of his life he would bend down to pick up from the ground any round or shiny things on which his failing eyes fell.

Hedgemustard was a good-natured man and in his book of sins there was nothing worse than lies, huge lies like childrens' stories.

"Once upon a time," he would say, "the English fleet came, and you should have seen me going off each night to comb the beach, because when there's a fleet in the ria the sea spits out good stuff. Ha, ha, ha. And so one night when the tide went out it left a really long box on the shore. And so I went and hoisted it on to my back. Ha, ha, ha. The bloody thing weighed so much it bent me double. But I got the strength from somewhere and managed to lug it up to my door. Ha, ha, ha. And so I called out to the wife. Open the door, Xoana, I've brought some treasure! Hurry up and open the door, woman, we're rich at last! Ha, ha, ha. I was puffing and blowing as I looked at the box full of all the riches I'd always longed for, and when Xoana came down we picked up the box and took it into the house. Ha, ha, ha. I'd be lying if I didn't say it was the happiest moment of my life. And so then we opened the box and as for finding something, well, we found something all right... do you know what it was? A dead Englishman. Ha, ha, ha."

Just like a badly painted wooden toy friar: he had a red nose, like that of a carnival mask, and a dried-up bald pate, like that of a shrivelled corpse, and you didn't know where to begin, mocking his shortcomings. Moody like bells that peal with festive madness one moment and toll for the dead the next. So fond of drinking that as a boy he went for the augardente from a bottled foetus, an uncle of his, and drank it dry. To earn a living he even stooped to howling like a dog in vineyards at harvest time.

But one day he ran into a woman on the way to a chapel in the fields. The woman was making good a vow, with a lamp in her hand. He spoke to her, he won her love, and they married straight away.

She is an ugly dwarf who earns her money at market selling old clothes. He has become a serious drunkard. And the two together are the laughing stock of the village on Sundays and holidays.

You should know that they had a son so strong in body and soul, so unlike his parents, that he seemed a stolen child. The boy grew up and became a worthy man and went away.

His father keeps saying:

"He isn't coming back, not with a mother like that..."

And his mother keeps saying:

"He isn't coming back, not with a father like that..."

But I know that he isn't coming back because he isn't rich enough yet to silence the laughter of the people who mock his parents; for with money you can become Your Excellency, as has happened before and will happen again.

The donkey didn't move a muscle; his eyes were wide open, fixed on the ground, and by the looks of it the donkey was thinking hard, sunk in his thoughts. I fixed my eyes on the donkey and I too started thinking, forgetting who I was; plunging into the depths of the donkey, and although I didn't realise it my thoughts were the donkey's thoughts.

Men don't want to be donkeys; instead they would like to be lions, tigers, wolves... precisely because men are bigger donkeys than lions, tigers, or wolves... and that is why to be called a donkey is offensive to men.

My back can bear any man yet men prefer a horse, an elephant... any beast bigger than them, so that nobody can say: "Look, there go two of a kind." They don't value us, because they see in us the virtues of good-hearted men.

We are the friends of the poor, the comfort of beggars; we have carried Our Lord and St Francis of Assisi on our backs; but never have we carried a warrior.

Peace will come when all men want to be donkeys.

They even went so far as to deny us brains because we walked at the side of the road. Fools! A donkey can be murdered by a motor car; but a donkey doesn't fall under a motor car as dogs and hens do... We sensed the arrival of motor cars before the devil in hell had invented them.

At this point I came round.

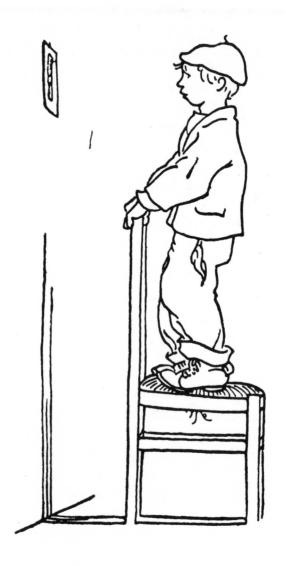

Migueliño's father was coming back from the Americas and the boy was bursting out of his Sunday suit with joy. Migueliño knew with his eyes shut what his father looked like; but before he left home he had a look at the portrait.

The *americanos* were getting off the boat. Migueliño and his mother were waiting on the quayside. The boy's heart was pounding against his chest-board and his eyes were searching the crowds for the father of his dreams.

Suddenly he sighted him in the distance. This was the man in the portrait, or even better turned-out, and Migueliño felt great love for him and the closer the *americano* came the more the boy longed to cover him with kisses. Alas, the *americano* walked past without a glance for anybody, and Migueliño didn't love him any more.

This time, this time it really was him! Migueliño sighted another very well-dressed man and his heart told him that this one was his father. The boy was longing to kiss him to death. He looked such a gentleman! Alas, the *americano* walked straight past and didn't even notice that a boy's anguished eyes were following him.

And so Migueliño chose many fathers who were not his father and he loved them all madly.

And as his searching grew more and more anguished he noticed that a man was hugging his mother. This was a man who didn't look like the one in the portrait: a skinny man, inside a baggy suit; a waxen man, with sticking-out ears, with hollow eyes, coughing...

This was Migueliño's father.

R omualdo was a *genteel* man. Thanks to his
stylish ways he gained a reputation as a well-
mannered man, although his hat-in-hand gestures did
not exactly have the stamp of the true fidalgo. For

Romualdo, so picky, so finicky, there was no manual trade that suited, and after endless whining he managed to get a foot in the door of the council offices, where he spent his life scribbling until the day of his passing. As well as a clerk Romualdo was a great wine taster, a skill his father had left him as inheritance.

In drinking it was the same as in writing: many tiny sips of wine daintily swallowed, tiny letters with tiny squiggly tails. As *genteel* at the office as in the bar. Romualdo often got drunk; but his legs never buckled. The more wine he had on board the more courteous he became.

Once Romualdo spent the night on the town and as he was arriving home he ran into some friends. It was Sunday.

"Come on, Romualdo, come with us, we're off to have an empanada for lunch."

"All right; but wait a second while I go and tell my wife."

And Romualdo went into his house. His friends heard a great commotion and then some furious words. Lazy bastard! Drunkard! Scum! Romualdo's wife was beating the man like somebody beating a drum. Bang bang! Bang bang!

Out came Romualdo straightening his clothes, and with an expression of feigned cheeriness he said to his friends:

"Let's get going, there's nobody home."

I n a church in the mountains I saw a man's skull serving as a collection box. It had a slit in its forehead and through there the good parishioners' money slipped.

A sacristy skull, pawed by hands stained with wax and oil, like the spine of an ancient missal, like the skin of an old tambourine. The poor human skull had been in service for many years, collecting money for the good of the souls in purgatory.

Now I am going to tell you something.

I know, because I know, that the skull belonged to a man who used to steal in a perfectly legal way by taking advantage of laws that protected him from the justice of our world.

But now the thief, in the world of truth, is condemned to receive the money he stole dropped on to his soul, ha'penny by ha'penny, farthing by farthing. His soul sits on the *Turkish Chair* of his sphenoid bone and every falling coin is a blow that it receives on its back.

It is chilling to think of so much suffering. The thief has been well punished now; but he still has to receive forty-seven thousand reás in copper coins.

I know, because…

R osendo's son would drift through the streets with his pallid ill-nourished young face. The three R's he had learnt were not enough for him to live off the work of his head and his hard-won gentility did not allow him to live off the work of his hands. He had done three years of secondary school and so he couldn't possibly work... And by dint of donated *ciggies* he was killing off the craving for the other joys of youth.

Rosendo's son yoked himself to a woman who was old, fat and rich, because ahead of him he could make out nothing but the bread of slavery. What a misfortune! For there is something worse than working so as not to die of hunger and that is getting married so as to be able to eat every day.

Rosendo's son went into marriage as a child goes into a basket of cakes, without seeing his misfortune, because he had not yet understood that the joy of eating when you are hungry ends in satiety and marriage ends only in death.

Rosendo's son got hold of some pesos on the days leading up to the wedding and when he married he had eight lottery tickets in the pockets of his new suit.

And once Rosendo's son was staring his misfortune in the face the lottery came along and placed in his hands many thousands of pesos that were not his wife's, that were his very own, for beyond all doubt he had them on him when he went to the church...

Fortune arrived late and now Rosendo's son always walks arm-in-arm with his wife, which is his tragedy.

He was a boy made of butter, pretty as a carnation. No lady could see him and not kiss him.

Dressed up like a fairytale prince, he had the baleful gaze of a boy raised among silks and kisses.

His exquisite outfits made of the boy a little doll to be kissed to death.

Each carnival outfit took two months to make, and his mother overflowed with joy.

For by his side all the other children looked pitiful, dressed in their cheap outfits.

And the child's beauty was his tragedy.

Little by little, in the warmth of caresses, the child became a young man. A young man full of goodness. A goodness full of innocence.

The young man entered a military academy and his mother wept and wept; but in the deepest depths of her soul she longed for her son to be different.

And when he came back dressed as a cadet his mother was mad with pride. And the young man still had that pure white goodness of his childhood.

One day the young man went off to war, as his profession demanded.

And there he fell mortally wounded. And as he died he said only these tremendously tragic words:

"Oh, Mummy!"

D on Froitoso does not take the paths that lead to
the truth, for he suspects that the truth has
certain similarities with death. Ever since his
contemporaries began growing bitter with
experience, Don Froitoso has turned his back on
them and befriended the young. A great optimist. The
day his legs can no longer hold up his body he will
call at the doctors' doors, and when he is left

stranded on his bed he will still be waiting for a miracle of science. Anything but come to terms with his old age.

Don Froitoso is one of those men who turn back the clock to turn back time and he closes his eyes when he does not want to be seen. All illusion and gentility, he is living out his last gasp as a gallant. A smooth-tongued gallant with his whiskers of flax and words like carnations in his mouth.

The bushy-bearded fidalgo has a spirit pure as a star. One day I said that nuns in convents were ugly and old and Don Froitoso glared at me and made me hold my tongue, because for this old gallant all the beautiful lies of Romanticism are still true.

Don Froitoso went to a dance last Antroido and there he met a servant girl in fancy dress. He treated her with great courtesy, without a trace of evil intent, without any foul language, as one should treat women… Don Froitoso paired up with the wench and together they went into a room, and there the old man began to recite poems by Bécquer, to which the servant girl listened laughing and laughing… And then the old man ordered champagne, top quality champagne. And two hours later the servant girl felt her head spinning, and grabbing on to Don Froitoso she said in dismay:

"Oh, that white wine and lemonade went down really badly!"

But that won't stop Don Froitoso from reciting poetry and ordering champagne at private dances.

D ear friend,

I used to be a thoughtful and reflective man whom Death the reaper stalked, teeth bared. The moment I closed my eyes, to go to sleep, a little finger of bone, or rather of ivory, would tap softly on my forehead and fear would explode within me. Every night.

I was dying of a bad heart and the doctors would not tell me the truth, for perhaps my illness had no cure. I visited one and another and another, and they all told me the same thing: *There is nothing wrong with you*. But I could feel my heart fluttering in its cage like a frantic bird, and only when I stayed still, not moving a muscle, would the bird in my breast go to sleep.

When the doctors were telling me *there is nothing wrong with you*, I could always glimpse in their eyes the flashing glint of lying and mockery, and one day my patience ran out and I spat in the specialist's face...

Since then I have been living in the Asylum.

Not long ago we were joined in this House by an eminent doctor whose expertise remains intact in spite of his madness, and I consulted him. He gave me a thorough examination and then told me with no hint of a lie in his eyes:

There's nothing wrong with your heart; you're mad, that's all.

So now I know I have a healthy heart, because mad doctors do not lie nor do they mock the sick. But... I have one doubt that chills me.

He said that I am mad, and now you, who walk free, must consult a lawyer about my case and he must tell you whether a mad doctor is entitled to know about madness.

Fondest regards from your friend,

X.

P.S. Please reply soon because I want to know whether I am mad or not.

This heap of stones and tiles, of rusty tin sheets and rotten boards, which looks like a tumbledown pigsty, was the den where old Fanchuca lived for many years.

This fig tree with its tangled branches gave shelter to her dwelling. As for the figs, nobody hungered for them, because they tasted of poverty.

Old Fanchuca went begging from door to door, back in those times when bread was more abundant in our villages than money. Those were the days when each gift of alms was kissed by the giver and kissed by the receiver: because alms were not bits of minted copper, but crusts of bread or cobs of maize.

Granny Fanchuca, being so poor and so old and so close to death, was beginning to turn into earth and could be mistaken from afar for the mud on the roads. But old Fanchuca knew how to do herself up on festa day by sewing many pretty patches on to her clothes: trimmings of her poverty, which year-round sun and rain were beginning to turn into earthen rags.

Old Fanchuca was over four score years old and on her clothes she wore the patches from all the festas, just as small birds wear their feathers.

The first example of poverty my eyes beheld was Granny Fanchuca and ever since then old age and destitution have been so closely associated in my memory that even today all wrinkly little old people look to me like door-to-door beggars.

The wizard of the mountain knows many ruses for healing wounded souls. He predicts all that is to come just by asking St Cyprian's Sieve, and he always has a suitable spell for every trouble. Oh yes, the wizard of the mountain knows more than he should.

One day it's a girl withering away from love and the wizard enquires of the sieve:

"Sieve that sieves the flour of Christianity: if So-and-so has his mind set on this girl then turn that way."

The sieve often turns the other way and the afflicted girl feels a deathly anguish; but the wizard, touched by all the love in the girl's tears, assures her that So-and-so will become blind to other women and will see nothing but her beauty. And then the spellbinding begins.

The wizard catches a toad and does many things to it and says many sayings to it, which he has learnt from the secret books; then, with a needle and green thread, he sews up its eyelids, without harming its pupils, and finally he speaks these words:

"Toad, little toad: you are a prisoner here and you shall not see sun or moon until So-and-so sets his mind on this fair girl."

And the girl leaves the wizard's house, her eyes shining with joy.

I saw him one stormy night by the light of a lightning bolt, exorcising the clouds, and I soon realised that the wizard has a spirit that comes from other ages, that he is a sage who was a poet once long ago.

The wizard was pushing at the clouds as if they were rams and shouting at them:

"To the sea, to the sea, to the sea with you, Thunder; to the sea, to the sea, for to sink and go under!"

The wizard defending the mountain.

D oña Florinda married *Cudgeller* and she lived
from one moon to another in hope of a baby
that did not come. Bemoaning her ill luck, Doña
Florinda would spend her empty hours on the

balcony, listening to the sorrowful clucking of the broody hens. *Cudgeller* was a gambler and he died of heart trouble, leaving the poor fidalga with her frustrated longing to caress a baby.

Mourning suited Doña Florinda and the white flesh of her arms attracted Don Roque's furtive glances. The good fidalga succeeded in awakening honourable love in the confirmed bachelor's heart and she managed to marry a second time. And once she was married her longing to be a mother returned, and again she lived from one moon to another in hope of a baby that never came. Don Roque departed from this world and Doña Florinda was left alone with her frustrated longing.

Many years have gone by. Today Doña Florinda is a little old lady sucked dry by time; so aged and so withered that she looks like a relic. Now, at the end of her long life — who would have thought it! — Doña Florinda can see her old longings fulfilled. Senility has made her believe she has a baby and any day now she will die of joy, of the joy of being a mother.

The poor fidalga keeps telling everybody:

"Didn't you know? I've had a baby."

And everybody bursts into laughter because people can no longer be moved.

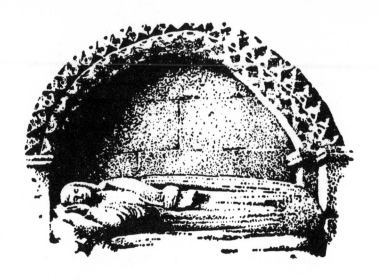

From the window in the tower the young Countess's tearful eyes are fixed on the last bend in the road, along which the joy she had known in love fled one day. With the worm of jealousy gnawing her heart away the young Countess is slowly dying in the window in the tower.

And days and months and years go by, as she scours the road for the return of her love. And one evening of tender thoughts, recalling that kiss they stole, the beautiful young Countess died of love.

This is how people tell of the death of the love-lorn maiden.

For hundreds of years this sarcophagus has held the ashes of the ill-fated young Countess, and the legend that is passed on from old to young has gathered sentimental strength thanks to this stone monument, a chest full of mystery for all romantic spirits.

Once it was opened by the town's *intellectuals* and inside they found bones, bits of linen, dust and... enough cherry stones to fill two bowls.

And the doctor, a man with large spectacles and a large amount of dandruff on his jacket, told the pharmacist:

"What the young Countess died of was a surfeit of cherries."

There are men who just can't keep quiet.

That boy who emerges from my childhood memories was a schoolmate of mine, a mortal enemy of cats and bold leader of all the tearaways. I cannot forget how he laughed as he threw stones at dead dogs to burst their bloated bellies.

Once our fearless schoolmate took us up to a beggar woman's shack and bragged:

"Watch this for a laugh."

Then he removed a bit of the roof and climbed into the shack. Soon crusts of bread and cobs of maize, alms that the old beggar woman had carried home like an ant that abundant autumn, came flying out through a window-hole. Then the tearaway appeared on the roof, laughing and laughing...

The pigs and the hens had a feast and we schoolboys watched wide-eyed, as if witnessing a sacrilege. We all stood motionless and when the tearaway noticed that our souls were shrinking inside us he said, to ease our pangs of conscience:

"After all, the old girl doesn't buy a thing, it's all given to her."

That boy is now a well-known and reputable gentleman, the owner of many millions, the master of many people and of many businesses out there in the Americas.

Heaven grant he never comes back.

S eñor Antón was alive when my grandfather was
a lad.

Señor Antón was a painter of great renown, and of
his craftsmanship there remain examples by the
score. Señor Antón painted everything in pretty
colours, covering pieces of wood and stone as if
dressing them up in their Sunday best. Señor Antón
believed that all things were naked if they were not

painted, and little by little he painted absolutely everything... turning stone into wood and wood into stone, to make people marvel. You think it's stone, eh? Well no sir, it's wood. You think it's wood, eh? Well no sir, it's stone. And there you have it, Señor Antón's artistic trickery.

His best works are some gardas civiles cut out of boards on the Holy Week float and a painting of souls in purgatory on the catafalque in church, where they say he had the old priest to a T; but Señor Antón made his living painting portraits.

How did Señor Antón paint portraits, you ask?

There he is with a jug of red wine in front of him and along comes a woman with a little girl. The woman says to Señor Antón:

"I should be most extremely grateful if you could paint a portrait of my little girl, because my husband is abroad, you see, and I should like to send him one."

Señor Antón casts an eye over the girl, then he places a hand on her head and moves it from side to side to scrutinise her face, and then he steps back a little to take her measure, half closing his eyes. Finally he squeezes her chin and replies:

"Next Saturday you can come for the portrait."

This is how Señor Antón painted portraits in the days when there were no photographers, and it is said that they all came out to a T.

I am going to tell you a sad story.

Shortly after she married, Doña Micaela started making little vests; but suddenly her hopes were destroyed and with tears in her eyes she put the spoilt fruit of her love into a jar of augardente.

Doña Micaela wrote on a little piece of paper: *Adolfo, 12th May 1887.* She stuck the piece of paper on the jar and after giving it a sorrowful kiss stored it away in the linen cupboard.

Don't laugh, because this is a sad story.

Before four months had passed Doña Micaela began working again on her vests. The good fidalga rejoiced to think about the heir who was on his way into the world, and for the second time Doña Micaela saw her hopes of motherhood dashed, and with deep sadness she put the latest fruit of her love into augardente.

Doña Micaela wrote: *Rosa, 7th January 1888.*

She stuck the piece of paper on the jar and with profound bitterness she stored it away in the linen cupboard.

Don't laugh, because this is a sad story.

Three times more the poor lady wept and into as many jars of augardente she put a Pedro, a Ramón and an Alicia.

Don't laugh.

The good fidalga realised that she would never caress a real child, and with a mother's devotion she dedicated her life to the loving care of those jars of augardente. Such a sad life!

No; don't laugh, because this is a sad case.

Whenever one of those frustrated dreams had a birthday Doña Micaela changed its augardente. Every day she would kiss the jars and tidy the little silk bows that girded the necks of the jars of Rosa and Alicia.

The good fidalga grew old and had such honest maids that they held the keys to the cupboards and managed the house.

One day one of the maids appeared before Doña Micaela. She was so distraught that she could not speak; but the poor girl threw herself on the floor and slowly sobbed out her confession:

"Forgive me, m'lady! Oh, what a disaster, ma'am! I dropped Master Adolfo and he broke."

And at that moment Doña Micaela lost heart for ever.

Glossary

Alalá: Traditional song in parts of northern Spain, made up of a chorus from which it takes its name, and octosyllabic verses.

Antroido: In Galicia, the traditional three-day period of fancy-dress, fireworks, parades, fun and general excess that precedes Lent.

Aturuxo: Shout of joy or encouragement made to accompany music or songs during festas.

Augardente: Galician 'firewater'. A highly alcoholic spirit made by distilling the grape refuse of the wine-making process.

Cruceiro: Monumental stone cross erected at cross-roads, roadsides, parish boundaries or churchyards, comprising a tall column that is supported by a stone platform into which steps are normally cut. Although they can be plain, cruceiros often have figures carved into them.

Empanada: Galicia's flat pies.

Festa: Party, entertainment, festival or fête.

Fidalgo (feminine *Fidalga*): Member of the petty rural Galician aristocracy; squire or seigneurial landlord.

Morriña: Longing for absent people or places, felt in Galicia in a particularly intense way because of the long history of emigration.

Muiñeira: Popular dance performed by one or more sets of partners.

Pazo: Country house or manorial dwelling of Galician aristocracy. Together with the church, the pazo was the nucleus of traditional rural Galician society.

Real (plural *Reás*): Spanish coin, now out of circulation, worth a quarter of a peseta.

Santa Compaña: In Galician folklore, procession of lost souls in purgatory that roams the night. A meeting with the Santa Compaña was seen as an augury of death.